This book belongs to …

....

OXFORD
UNIVERSITY PRESS

Great Clarendon Street,
Oxford, OX2 6DP, United Kingdom

Oxford University Press is a department of the University of Oxford.
It furthers the University's objective of excellence in research, scholarship,
and education by publishing worldwide. Oxford is a registered trade mark
of Oxford University Press in the UK and in certain other countries

British Library Cataloguing in Publication Data Data available

978-0-19-831028-0

1 3 5 7 9 10 8 6 4 2

Paper used in the production of this book is a natural, recyclable product
made from wood grown in sustainable forests. The manufacturing
process conforms to the environmental regulations of the country of origin.

Printed in China.

Acknowledgements:

Series Editors: Kate Ruttle, Annemarie Young

READ WITH
Biff,
Chip &
Kipper

The Golden Touch
and Other Stories

OXFORD
UNIVERSITY PRESS

Tips for Reading Together

Children learn best when reading is fun.

- Talk about the title and the pictures on the front cover and the title pages of each story.

- Identify the letter patterns *ear* and *eer* in the title and talk about the sound they make when you read them.

- Look at the words on page 8. Say the sounds in each word and then say the word (e.g. *g-ear, h-ere, p-ier, sh-eer*).

- Read the story and find the words with the letter patterns *ear, ere, eer* and *ier*.

- Talk about the story and do the fun activity at the end of the story.

Children enjoy re-reading stories and this helps to build their confidence.

Have fun!

After you have read the story, find the ten seagulls in the pictures.

The main sound practised in this book is 'ear' as in *near*.

 For more hints and tips on helping your child become a successful and enthusiastic reader look at our website www.oxfordowl.co.uk.

Change Gear! Steer!

Written by Roderick Hunt
Illustrated by Nick Schon,
based on the original characters
created by Roderick Hunt and Alex Brychta

OXFORD

UNIVERSITY PRESS

Read these words

h**ere**

ve**ere**d

n**ear**ly

sh**eer**

p**ier**

sev**ere**

cl**ear**

che**ere**d

Nearly every year Nadim and his
dad went to the seaside.

Nadim liked to go to the arcade with his dad. The arcade was on the pier.

"They have really exciting games
in here," said Nadim.

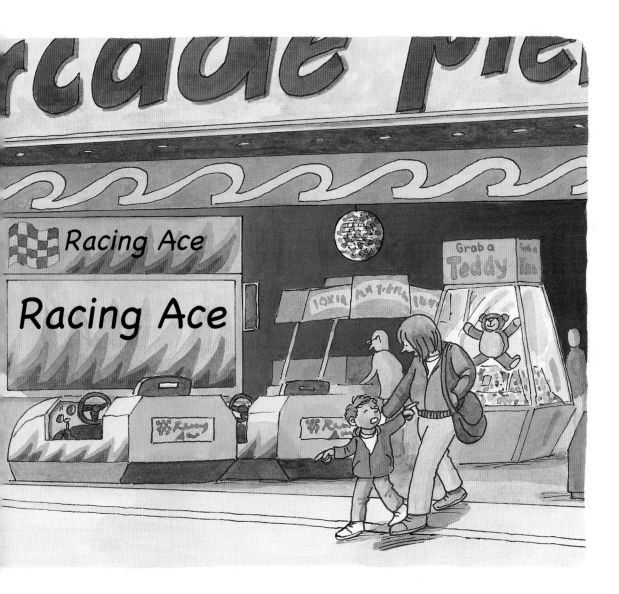

Nadim saw a game called Racing Ace.
"Wow!" said Nadim. "Let's race here."

"Yes, let's race," said Nadim's dad.

"But one thing is clear. I'm an ace racer."

The screen said ...

Nadim chose one with a rear spoiler.

Nadim's dad chose a blue car.

It had three gears like Nadim's.

Nadim could hear a cheer from the crowd.
He gripped the steering wheel.

The light went green.

The screen said … GO!

"We're off," yelled Nadim's dad.
He shot off so fast that his car spun
off at the first bend.

Nadim's car was hard to steer.
It veered to the right but he got past
his dad.

The road went up a steep hill. It came to a sharp bend.

"I must not brake too hard," said Nadim,
"in case I spin off like Dad."

Brake.
Change gear.
Steer.

The road went down a mountain.
It had a sheer drop on one side.

Nadim slowed down for another bend.
"Here I come!" yelled Nadim's dad.

Nadim's dad nearly hit the rear of Nadim's car. He shot past but he took the bend too fast.

The car spun round and shot off
the road.

"Hard luck, Dad," said Nadim.

The road went into a forest. Nadim came to a clearing. Oh no! It was a dead end.

Nadim had to turn and go back.

"Hard luck, Nadim," said his dad.

The race was almost over, but Nadim just had to get past his dad. He could see the final bend.

Nadim took a risk. He saw a gap and put his foot down. He cut the corner at speed and shot past.

Nadim had won the race.
The crowd cheered.

"Oh dear!" said Nadim's dad. "I nearly did it. Well done, Nadim."

"Let's come here again," said Nadim.
"Yes, but you won't win next time,"
said his dad.

Talk about the story

Why did Nadim like going to the arcade on the pier?

Who thought they would win, Nadim or Dad?

Why was Nadim careful not to brake too hard?

What games do you like to play?

Because There was a race game

Dad

So he won't spin in the corner

Memory

33

Maze

Help Nadim win the car rally and get to the finish line.

FINISH

Tips for Reading Together

Children learn best when reading is fun.

- Talk about the title and the pictures on the front cover and the title pages of each story.

- Identify the letter patterns *air*, *are* and *ear* in the title and talk about the sound they make when you read them.

- Look at the *air*, *are*, *ear* and *ere* words on page 38. Say the sounds in each word and then say the word (e.g. *air – hair*, *air – chair*).

- Read the story and find the words with the letter patterns *air*, *are*, *ear* and *ere*.

- Talk about the story and do the fun activity at the end of the story.

Children enjoy re-reading stories and this helps to build their confidence.

Have fun!

After you have read the story, find the ten buttons in the pictures.

The main sound practised in this book is 'air' as in *pair* and *hair*.

For more hints and tips on helping your child become a successful and enthusiastic reader look at our website www.oxfordowl.co.uk.

A Rare Pair of Bears

Written by Roderick Hunt
Illustrated by Nick Schon,
based on the original characters
created by Roderick Hunt and Alex Brychta

OXFORD
UNIVERSITY PRESS

Read these words

hair   wh**ere**

b**ear**   sp**are**

ch**air**   c**are**

th**ere**   w**ear**

Gran had an old photo of a little
girl with long, fair hair.
"Who is she, Gran?" asked Biff.

"She was my great grandmother,"
said Gran. "She was called Mary."

Biff stared at the photo. On a little
chair next to Mary was a toy bear.
"I've still got that bear," said Gran.

Gran went upstairs to her spare room
and found a box. Inside the box was
the bear in the photo.

He's called Gordon.

"He's had a lot of wear," said Biff.
"There's a bare patch on his back and
a tear in his tummy."

"That's not all," said Gran. She took another bear out of the box. "This bear is called Ernest."

"These old bears are quite rare,"
said Dad. "They could be worth a lot
of money."

A pair of bears.
Wow!

There was a toy fair in town. Dad and Gran took Biff, Chip and Kipper.

Gran had her two bears in a bag.
"Let's see how much they are worth,"
she said.

Gran took her bears to an expert.
"Oh my," the expert said. "This is a
fairly rare pair of bears."

"Ernest is worth thousands of pounds. Gordon has a tear in his tummy. He is worth a little less."

They went round the toy fair.

"I like this old airship," said Biff.

Gran put her bag down on a chair.
"Did all dolls wear boots like these?"
asked Kipper.

"This is good," said Chip. "I can see over the top of Dad."

Chip looked in the periscope. He saw
a woman take Gran's bag with the
bears.

Gran went to pick up her bag.
"Oh no!" gasped Gran. "My bears
have been stolen."

Gran was upset.

"This is a nightmare," she said.

"I saw who stole the bears," said Chip.
"She had black hair and a red coat."

"Look!" said Biff. "There she is. She's getting away."

Gran began to run.

"I'll soon get her," she said.

"Be careful, Gran," called Dad.

The woman ran but Gran was much quicker.

"Got you," she said.

59

Dad was cross. "You gave us such a scare," he said. "You must take more care at your age."

A week later, Gran came to Biff and
Chip's house. "I am the good fairy,"
she said.

"I sold the bears," said Gran, "and now
I want to share the money with you all."

Talk about the story

Why did Gran take the bears to the Toy Fair?

How did Chip help Gran catch the thief?

Why did Gran say she was the good fairy?

What old toys do you have?

Maze

Help Gran to catch the thief.

Tips for Reading Together

Children learn best when reading is fun.

- Talk about the title and the pictures on the cover and the title pages of each story.

- Discuss what you think the story might be about.

- Read the story together, inviting your child to read as much of it as they can.

- Give lots of praise as your child reads, and help them when necessary.

- Try different ways of helping if they get stuck on a word. For example, get them to say the first sound of the word, or break it into chunks, or read the whole sentence again. Focus on the meaning.

- Re-read the story later, encouraging your child to read as much of it as they can.

Have fun!

Children enjoy re-reading stories and this helps to build their confidence.

> After you have read the story, find the ten mice hidden in the pictures.

> This book includes these useful common words:
> called   children   might   suddenly

For more hints and tips on helping your child become a successful and enthusiastic reader look at our website www.oxfordowl.co.uk.

The Palace Statues

Written by Cynthia Rider,
based on the original characters
created by Roderick Hunt and Alex Brychta
Illustrated by Alex Brychta

OXFORD
UNIVERSITY PRESS

The children put on a play called
The Golden Statue. Chip was the statue.
He had on a golden cloak and gold
face paint.

"I like this gold face paint," said
Anneena.

The magic key began to glow.

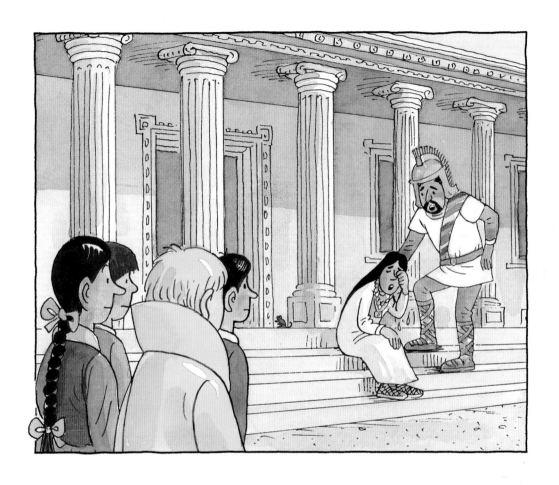

The magic took the children to a
palace. They saw a man talking to
a girl.

"Don't cry, Eva," he said.

"What's the matter?" asked Biff.

"This is my brother, Aran," said
Eva. "He guards the golden statues
in the palace."

"The statues all have jewels," said
Aran. "But someone is stealing the
jewels, and I *must* catch the robber."

Aran showed the children the golden statues. "The robber might steal more jewels tonight," he said. "What can I do?"

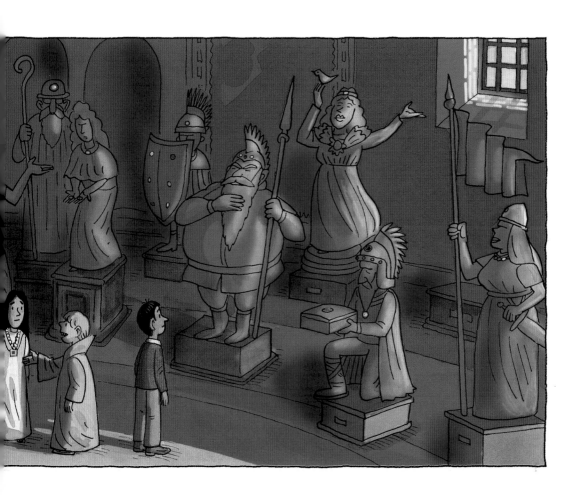

Chip had an idea. "You can
dress up as a golden statue," he said.
"Then you can keep watch."

That night, Aran dressed up as a
golden statue.

"I'm glad we've got this gold face
paint," said Anneena.

Aran went into the statue room.

He stood in the deepest shadows.

"You need a jewel," said Eva. She

gave him her necklace, and went out.

Suddenly, a secret door slid open.
Two men crept into the room. They
took the rest of the jewels.

One of the men spotted Aran.
"I didn't see that statue last night,"
he said. "Let's get that necklace."

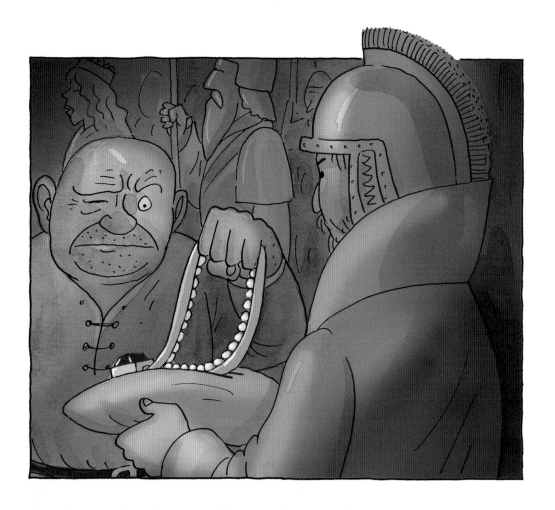

Aran held his breath as the man grabbed the necklace.

At last, he heard a soft thud as the secret door slid shut.

Aran called
the children. He
showed them the secret
door. They all crept down
some steps and along a shadowy tunnel.

Suddenly, Biff tripped and fell.

"Who's there?" shouted the men.

"Run!" whispered Nadim. "Hide under the steps."

A robber came up to the steps.
He held up his lamp but the
children were as still as statues.

"There's nobody here," he said.

The men went into a dusty room. The children followed them and peeped round the door.

"There's another door!" said Aran.
"It must lead into the palace garden.
They might escape through that."

"I know what we can do," said
Nadim, and he told the others his
plan.

"That's a good idea," said Eva.

Eva raced back up the steps.
She told the guards to go to the
garden door. Then she ran back to
the others.

Aran marched stiffly into the
dusty room.

"Give me back my necklace!" he
roared, in a voice like thunder.

The robbers jumped up.

"Help! The statue is alive!" they
screamed. They raced out of the
garden door . . .

. . . and ran right into the guards!

The next day, Aran and Eva gave
the children a golden statue.

"Thank you for helping us," they
said. The magic key began to glow.

The magic took the children home.

"The statue looks just like Eva,"
said Nadim.

"Yes," said Chip. "And Anneena
looks just like the statue!"

Talk about the story

Why was
Eva crying?

What was
Nadim's plan?

How do you
think the children
felt when they
were hiding?

How would you
help someone who
was crying?

Picture puzzle

Help Aran to match the jewels to the statues.

Tips for Reading Together

Children learn best when reading is fun.

- Talk about the title and the pictures on the cover and the title pages of each story.
- Discuss what you think the story might be about.
- Read the story together, inviting your child to read as much of it as they can.
- Give lots of praise as your child reads, and help them when necessary.
- Try different ways of helping if they get stuck on a word. For example, get them to say the first sound of the word, or break it into chunks, or read the whole sentence again. Focus on the meaning.
- Re-read the story later, encouraging your child to read as much of it as they can.

Children enjoy re-reading stories and this helps to build their confidence.

Have fun!

After you have read the story, find all the fruit hidden in the pictures.

This book includes these useful common words:
asked   children   chocolate   everything

For more hints and tips on helping your child become a successful and enthusiastic reader look at our website www.oxfordowl.co.uk.

The
Golden Touch

Written by Roderick Hunt
Illustrated by Alex Brychta

OXFORD
UNIVERSITY PRESS

The children were dipping
strawberries into chocolate.
"They look yummy!" said Chip.
"They taste yummy!" said Kipper.

Kipper went to Biff's room. He had
chocolate on his hands. He got
chocolate on everything he touched.

"Go away, Kipper!" said Biff.

"You're getting chocolate on everything," said Chip.

"I wish everything I touched turned into chocolate," said Kipper.

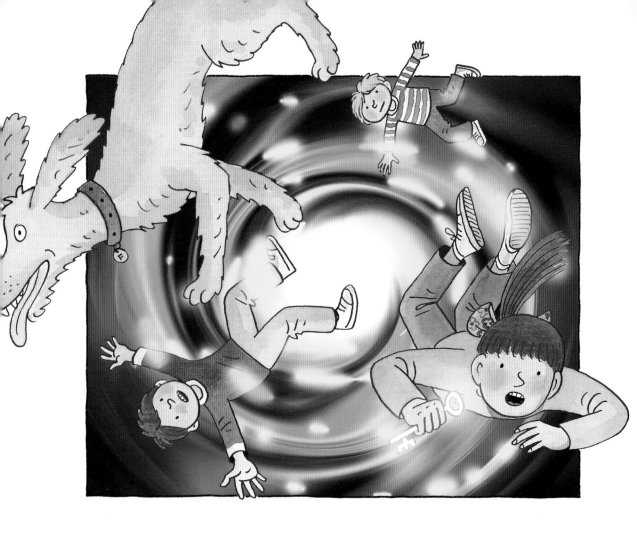

"That's just greedy," said Chip.

Just then the magic key began to glow. It took the children into an adventure.

They saw a girl sitting by a river.

She was crying.

"What's the matter?" asked Biff.

"Come with me and I'll show you,"
said the girl. "My name is Zoe."
Zoe took them to a palace.

The children gasped. The palace
was made of gold, and a gold tree
stood outside.

Zoe took the children inside.
Everything was made of gold, even
the food on the table!

"My father is King Midas," said
Zoe sadly. "He made a wish that
everything he touched turned into
gold. Now his wish has come true!"

"If the food turns into gold, how can he eat it?" asked Chip.

"He can't," said Zoe. "And if he touches me, I'll turn into gold too."

Just then King Midas came in.
Zoe hid behind Biff. "My father
used to hug me," she said, "but he
mustn't do it anymore."

King Midas saw Floppy. "I love dogs,"
he said. "Come here!"

"Stop!" called Chip. "Don't touch
that dog!"

It was too late. King Midas patted
Floppy and turned Floppy into gold.

"I'm so sorry," said King Midas.
"I forgot that everything I touch
turns into gold. I wish I could turn
him back into a real dog again."

"Who granted the wish?" asked Biff.

"It was Dionysus," said the king.

"Then we must go and see him," said Biff, "and ask him to help."

Dionysus lived on Mount Olympus.
It was a long way to walk, but at last
King Midas and the children arrived.

"Why have you come back to see
me?" asked Dionysus.

"I have come to ask you to
help me," said King Midas.

"I want everything back the way
it was," said King Midas. "My wish
was silly."

"You were foolish and greedy,"
said Dionysus. "But you have learnt
your lesson. Now go back and do
what I tell you."

Dionysus told them to get water
from the river. They had to pour it
onto everything that had turned
into gold.

"It works!" said King Midas. "I'm
so glad your dog is back."
"So am I!" said Kipper.

King Midas gave Zoe a hug.

"What a fool I have been," he said.

"I'm glad I can hug you now. I will
never ask for gold again!"

King Midas looked at the children.
"Thank you for helping us," he said.

The key began to glow. It was
time to go home.

"Hey! Why did you do that?"
asked Kipper, crossly.

"To stop you from turning into
chocolate," laughed Chip.

Talk about the story

Why was Zoe crying?

How was Floppy turned into gold?

Why was King Midas's wish foolish and greedy?

What would you wish for?

Picture puzzle

Match each water carrier with his gold twin.